Eyeless
the
Corona
Virus

Katie Burtenshaw

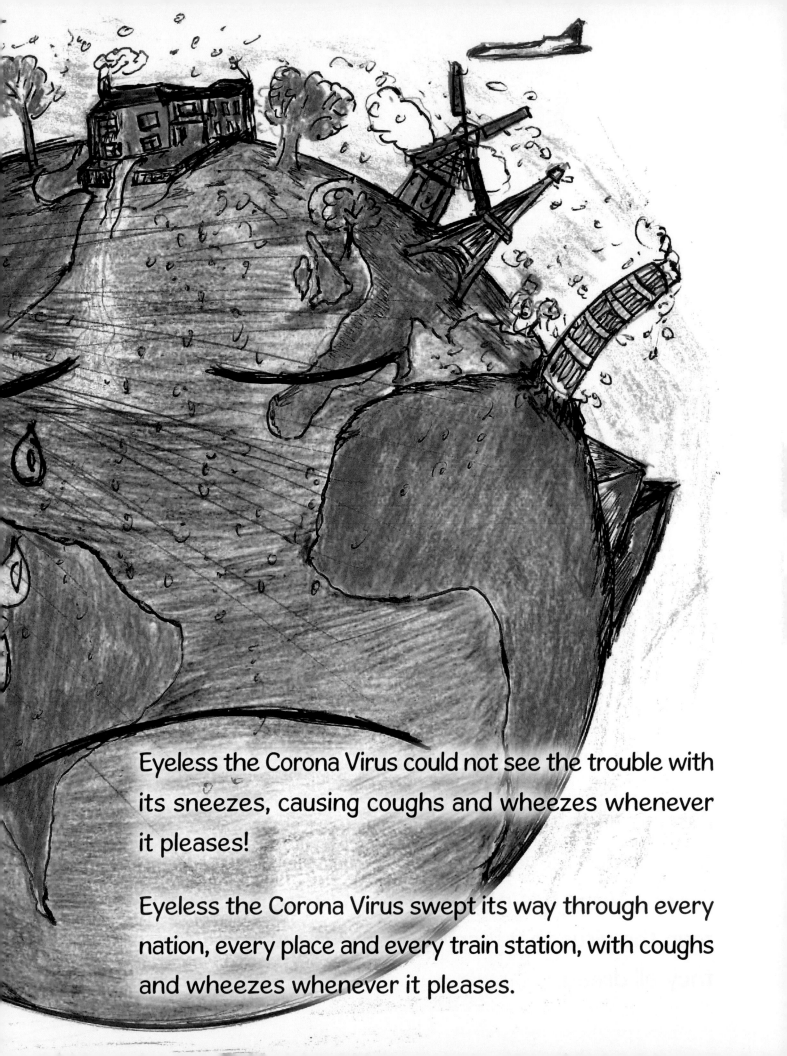

Eyeless the Corona Virus could not see the trouble with its sneezes, causing coughs and wheezes whenever it pleases!

Eyeless the Corona Virus swept its way through every nation, every place and every train station, with coughs and wheezes whenever it pleases.

It travels everywhere oblivious of the scare, not knowing it was wrong, it even chewed up all the toilet roll as it went along!

Forcing all the people to stay indoors, so not to catch its germy spores. Eyeless the Corona Virus has no idea why the people fear, the virus that it spreads, or the fever they all dread.

It continued to spread its germy spores keeping the people stuck indoors. It kept them away from everyone close to their heart; which made them feel worlds apart.

Still Eyeless the Corona Virus can't see the trouble
it is making, leaving us all quaking.....with its coughs
and wheezes whenever it pleases!

The very clever doctors and scientists knew they had to be quick to stop the people getting sick. They needed to get Eyeless the Corona Virus to see the trouble it is making, leaving us all quaking...with its coughs and wheezes whenever it pleases.

The very clever doctors and scientists said,
"Right we know what to do. We can make it
shoo!"

"Use a tissue to catch its coughs and sneezes
and great big wheezes. Then put it in the bin.
That will get rid of "im"".

Still Eyeless the Corona Virus can't see the trouble it is making, leaving us all quaking.....with its coughs and wheezes whenever it pleases!

The very clever doctors and scientists knew they had to be quick to stop the people getting sick.They needed to get Eyeless the Corona Virus to see the trouble it is making, leaving us all quaking...with its coughs and wheezes whenever it pleases.

The very clever doctors and scientists said "Right we know what to do. We can make it shoo!"

STOP! STOP! STOP!

We need to make a stand ...catch its coughs and sneezes and great big wheezes in your hand."

Then you have to

WASH! WASH! WASH!

your hands well.

That will work, if you do that for a spell.

Still Eyeless the Corona Virus can't see the trouble it is making, leaving us all quaking.....with its coughs and wheezes whenever it pleases!

The very clever doctors and scientists knew they had to be quick to stop the people getting sick. They needed to get Eyeless the Corona Virus to see the trouble it was making, leaving us all quaking...with its coughs and wheezes whenever it pleases.

The clever scientist and doctors said, "Right we know what to do to make it shoo!"

"We will find a vaccination for every person in every nation and that's what we must do for the whole population.

The clever scientists and doctors were relentless in working, to find a vaccination for every person in every nation. They worked day and night for weeks and months, never pausing in finding a way to make Eyeless the Corona Virus see the trouble it was causing.

In the meantime the people waited and waited, stayed safe and never congregated. It seemed to take forever but they knew the doctors and scientists were clever.

Then over time with very hard work from the clever scientists and doctors, with the help from every person from every nation, being cool and following the rules; Wash your hands.... Cover your face and when you meet other people.... Make lots of space!

They will find a vaccination that will help Eyeless the Corona Virus to see the trouble it is making, leaving us all quaking... with its coughs and wheezes whenever it pleases.

Then when it stops spreading its germy spores that kept us indoors. We won't have to be smart and stand 2 meters apart. We won't have to wear masks, that are hot and sticky and "Phew" can smell quite "Icky".

We can go back normal and stop being so formal.

We can finally make the most of being close, with all our family and friends again, in the sun and the moon.

Let's hope it's very soon!

About the Author

I am a mother of six and a grandmother of five, I have worked with the under 5's for over 30 years and I am currently the Operational Manager of an Outstanding Early Years Provision

As soon as the Covid-19 crisis started to affect our lives, it became very apparent to me the sudden changes to our young children's lives could have an immediate and lasting impact on our children's wellbeing.

Since the start of the pandemic, it was very clear, that there was a unilateral sense amongst parents that the children were struggling to understand all the sudden changes to their lives and consequently the parents needed a simplistic and fun way of explaining this new way of life to their children. I quickly became determined to find a way to conceptualize the Coronavirus into a character that children could relate too.

Eyeless the Corona Virus uses fun and witty illustrations and text to teach children how to stay safe, by protecting themselves and others from the Coronavirus and by helping children make links to this new way of life and gain a better understanding of the current world around them.

AuthorHouse™ UK
1663 Liberty Drive
Bloomington, IN 47403 USA
www.authorhouse.co.uk
UK TFN: 0800 0148641 (Toll Free inside the UK)
UK Local: 02036 956322 (+44 20 3695 6322 from outside the UK)

Because of the dynamic nature of the Internet, any web addresses or links contained in this book may have changed since publication and may no longer be valid. The views expressed in this work are solely those of the author and do not necessarily reflect the views of the publisher, and the publisher hereby disclaims any responsibility for them.

Any people depicted in stock imagery provided by Getty Images are models, and such images are being used for illustrative purposes only.
Certain stock imagery © Getty Images.

This book is printed on acid-free paper.

ISBN: 978-1-7283-5677-8 (sc)
ISBN: 978-1-7283-5676-1 (e)

Print information available on the last page.

Published by AuthorHouse 10/14/2020

authorHOUSE

Printed in the United States
By Bookmasters